Ella's Games

For my daughter, Isobel.
D.B.

For Luke and Hayley
and all the games we've played.
With love, P.K.

Scholastic Children's Books,
Commonwealth House, 1-19 New Oxford Street,
London WC1A 1NU, UK
a division of Scholastic Ltd

London – New York – Toronto – Sydney – Auckland
Mexico City – New Delhi – Hong Kong

First published in hardback by Scholastic Ltd, 2002
This paperback edition published by Scholastic Ltd, 2002

Text copyright © David Bedford, 2002
Illustrations copyright © Peter Kavanagh, 2002

ISBN 0 439 98273 1

Printed and bound by Oriental Press, Dubai, UAE
All rights reserved

2 4 6 8 10 9 7 5 3 1

Ella's Games

David Bedford

Illustrated by Peter Kavanagh

Ella's brothers played all morning in the honeysuckle tub. Ella wanted to play too. "You'd be scared!" said Jack. "You're too small!" said Jim. "You can't even climb!" said Joe.

So Ella went away
to play on her own,
and found . . .

a cat's whisker.

And she made up a game.

"What's that?"
asked Jack when
Ella came back.
"I'll tell you . . ."
said Ella.

"It's a whisker from a rainbow cat, who tried to chase me. But I didn't run. I plucked out one of her whiskers, and frightened her away!"

MIAOW!

"Can I play in the honeysuckle tub now?" asked Ella. "I won't be scared – I can frighten cats!" "You still can't play with us," said Jim, "because you're too small."

So Ella went away to play
on her own again, and
found . . .

a fluffy dandelion.

And she made up a game.

Ella's brothers were having a bath
when Ella came back.
"Why are you so muddy?" asked Jim.
"I'll tell you . . ." said Ella.

"I found an elephant having a mud bath.
He said, 'Help me, Ella, I'm stuck!'
So I tickled his nose with a feathery flower,
and he sniffed and snuffled and SNEEZED
his way out."

ATTISHOO!

"*Now* can I play in the honeysuckle tub?"
asked Ella. "It doesn't matter if I'm small
– I can save elephants!"
"You still can't play with us," said Joe.
"You can't climb."

So Ella went away to play
on her own once more,
and found . . .

a big stone.

And she made up a game.

Ella's brothers were getting
ready for bed when
Ella came back.
"What's that?" asked Joe.
"I'll tell you . . ." said Ella.

"It's a dragon's sore tooth.
I climbed all the way up to the
dragon's head, and plucked it out.
He was so pleased, he took me
flying round and round the clouds."

"Wow!" said Joe. "You play all
the *best* games, Ella."

That night, Ella's brothers couldn't sleep.
"Ella," asked Jack, "will you play in the
honeysuckle tub tomorrow? You won't be
scared – you frightened a cat!"
"You're not too small," said Jim. "You saved
an elephant!"
"And you *can* climb," said Joe. "You even
climbed a dragon!"

"All right," said Ella happily.
"What shall we play?" asked Jack, Jim and Joe.
"I'll tell you . . ." said Ella.

And the next day, Jack,
Jim and Joe made ready
to sail across the sea

in the fantastic new
adventure of . . .

Captain Ella
and her brave
pirate crew!